Also by Myra Cohn Livingston

CELEBRATIONS

THE CHILD AS POET:
MYTH OR REALITY?

A CIRCLE OF SEASONS

EARTH SONGS

SEA SONGS

SKY SONGS

SPACE SONGS

A SONG I SANG TO YOU

COME AWAY

HIGGLEDY-PIGGLEDY:
VERSES AND PICTURES

A LOLLYGAG OF LIMERICKS

MONKEY PUZZLE AND OTHER POEMS

NO WAY OF KNOWING:
DALLAS POEMS

O SLIVER OF LIVER AND OTHER POEMS

THE WAY THINGS ARE AND OTHER POEMS

THERE WAS A PLACE AND OTHER POEMS

WORLDS I KNOW AND OTHER POEMS

(Margaret K. McElderry Books)

Edited by Myra Cohn Livingston

HOW PLEASANT TO KNOW MR. LEAR!

POEMS OF LEWIS CARROLL

THESE SMALL STONES

———————————

CALLOOH! CALLAY!

HOLIDAY POEMS FOR YOUNG READERS

O FRABJOUS DAY!

POETRY FOR HOLIDAYS AND SPECIAL OCCASIONS

POEMS OF CHRISTMAS

WHY AM I GROWN SO COLD?

POEMS OF THE UNKNOWABLE

A LEARICAL LEXICON

I LIKE YOU, IF YOU LIKE ME

(Margaret K. McElderry Books)

DILLY DILLY PICCALILLI

Poems for the Very Young

chosen by

Myra Cohn Livingston

illustrated by

Eileen Christelow

Margaret K. McElderry Books
NEW YORK

For Matthew Terry Marks,
Tommy Magimper,
and Uncle Lee

Margaret K. McElderry Books
Macmillan Publishing Company
866 Third Avenue,
New York, NY 10022
Collier Macmillan Canada, Inc.

Designed by Barbara A. Fitzsimmons

Printed in the United States of America
First Edition
10   9   8   7   6   5   4   3   2   1

Library of Congress Cataloging-in-Publication Data
Dilly dilly piccalilli/chosen by Myra Cohn Livingston.—1st ed.
p.   cm.
Summary: A collection of poems about such topics as bugs, weather,
food, and the sea, by poets ranging from Robert Louis Stevenson and
Walter de la Mare to Gwendolyn Brooks and Arnold Lobel.
ISBN 0-689-50466-7
1. Children's poetry, American. 2. Children's poetry, English.
[1. American poetry—Collections. 2. English poetry—Collections.]
I. Livingston, Myra Cohn.
PS586.3.D55   1989   811'.008'09282—dc19   88—23005   CIP AC

ACKNOWLEDGMENTS

The editor and publisher thank the following for permission to reprint the copyrighted material listed below:

Curtis Brown, Ltd., for "April" from *Everett Anderson's Year* by Lucille Clifton. Reprinted by permission of Curtis Brown, Ltd. Copyright © 1974 by Lucille Clifton.

Dodd, Mead & Company, Inc., for "Calico Pie," "The Owl and the Pussycat," and "The Table and the Chair" by Edward Lear.

Doubleday, a division of Bantam Doubleday Dell Publishing Group, Inc., for "I'd Like to Be a Lighthouse" from the book *Taxis and Toadstools* by Rachel Field. Copyright © 1926 by Doubleday. Reprinted by permission of Doubleday, a division of Bantam Doubleday Dell Publishing Group, Inc. "The Lamb" from the book *The Collected Poems of Theodore Roethke* by Theodore Roethke. Published by Doubleday, a division of Bantam Doubleday Dell Publishing Group, Inc.

E. P. Dutton for "Solitude" from *Now We Are Six* by A. A. Milne. Copyright © 1927 by E. P. Dutton, renewed 1955 by A. A. Milne. Reprinted by permission of the publisher, E. P. Dutton, a division of NAL Penguin, Inc.

James Emanuel for "A Small Discovery," copyright © 1972.

Harcourt Brace Jovanich, Inc., for "Potomac Town in February" from *Smoke and Steel* by Carl Sandburg, copyright © 1920 by Harcourt Brace Jovanovich, Inc.; renewed 1948 by Carl Sandburg. Reprinted by permission of the publisher.

Contents

The Lamb

The Lamb just says, I AM!
He frisks and whisks, *He* can.
He jumps all over. Who
Are *you*? You're jumping too!

Theodore Roethke

1

Uptown, downtown,
Wrong side to,
Goodness me
What a hullabaloo!

Upstairs, downstairs,
Roundabout,
Backwards, forwards,
Inside OUT!

Clyde Watson

Around My Room

I put on a pair of overshoes
And walk around my room,
With my Father's bamboo walking stick,
And my Mother's feather broom.

I walk and walk and walk and walk,
I walk and walk around.
I love my Father's tap-tap-tap,
My Mother's feathery sound.

William Jay Smith

The Table and The Chair

Said the Table to the Chair,
"You can hardly be aware
How I suffer from the heat
And from chilblains on my feet.
If we took a little walk,
We might have a little talk;
Pray let us take the air,"
Said the Table to the Chair.

Said the Chair unto the Table,
"Now, you *know* we are not able:
How foolishly you talk,
When you know we *cannot* walk!"
Said the Table with a sigh,
"It can do no harm to try.
I've as many legs as you:
Why can't we walk on two?"

So they both went slowly down,
And walked about the town
With a cheerful bumpy sound
As they toddled round and round;

And everybody cried,
As they hastened to their side,
"See! the Table and the Chair
Have come out to take the air!"

But in going down an alley
To a castle in the valley,
They completely lost their way,
And wandered all the day;
Till, to see them safely back,
They paid a Ducky-quack,
And a Beetle, and a Mouse,
Who took them to their house.

Then they whispered to each other,
"O delightful little brother,
What a lovely walk we've taken!
Let us dine on beans and bacon."
So the Ducky and the leetle
Browny-Mousy and the Beetle
Dined and danced upon their heads
Till they toddled to their beds.

Edward Lear

Up the Hill

Hippety-Hop, goes the Kangaroo,
And the big brown Owl goes, Hoo-Hoo-Hoo!
Hoo-Hoo-Hoo and Hippety-Hop,
Up the Hill, and over the Top!

Baa-Baa-Baa, goes the little white Lamb,
And the Gate that is stuck goes, Jim-Jam-Jam!
Jim-Jam-Jam and Baa-Baa-Baa,
Here we go down again, Tra-La-La!

William Jay Smith

The Swing

How do you like to go up in a swing,
    Up in the air so blue?
Oh, I do think it the pleasantest thing
    Ever a child can do!

Up in the air and over the wall,
    Till I can see so wide,
Rivers and trees and cattle and all
    Over the countryside—

Till I look down on the garden green,
    Down on the roof so brown—
Up in the air I go flying again,
    Up in the air and down!

Robert Louis Stevenson

Hello and Good-Bye

Hello and good-bye
Hello and good-bye

When I'm in a swing
Swinging low and then high,
Good-bye to the ground
Hello to the sky.

Hello to the rain
Good-bye to the sun,
Then hello again sun
When the rain is all done.

In blows the winter,
Away the birds fly.
Good-bye and hello
Hello and good-bye.

Mary Ann Hoberman

The Sun

I told the Sun that I was glad,
I'm sure I don't know why;
Somehow the pleasant way he had
Of shining in the sky,
Just put a notion in my head
That wouldn't it be fun
If, walking on the hill, I said
"I'm happy" to the Sun.

John Drinkwater

Numbers

When I can count the numbers far,
And know all the figures that there are,

Then I'll know everything, and I
Can know about the ground and sky,

And all the little bugs I see,
And I'll count the leaves on the silver-leaf tree,
And all the days that ever can be.

I'll know all the cows and sheep that pass,
And I'll know all the grass,

And all the places far away,
And I'll know everything some day.

Elizabeth Madox Roberts

Bugs

I am very fond of bugs.
I kiss them
And I give them hugs.

Karla Kuskin

Tea Party

Mister Beedle Baddlebug,
Don't bandle up in your boodlebag
Or numble in your jimblejug,
Now eat your nummy tiffletag
Or I will never invite you
To tea again with me. Shoo!

Harry Behn

Firefly

A little light is going by,
Is going up to see the sky,
A little light with wings.

I never could have thought of it,
To have a little bug all lit
And made to go on wings.

Elizabeth Madox Roberts

Move Over

Big
burly
bumblebee
buzzing
through the grass,
move over.

Black and
yellow
clover rover,
let me pass.

Fat and
furry
rumblebee
loud on the
wing,
let me
hurry
past
your sting.

Lilian Moore

The Grasshopper

Down
a
deep
well
a
grasshopper
fell.

By kicking about
He thought to get out.
He might have known better,
For that got him wetter.
To kick round and round
Is the way to get drowned,
And drowning is what
I should tell you he got.
But
the
well
had
a
rope
that
dangled

15

some
hope.

And sure as molasses
On one of his passes
He found the rope handy
And up he went, *and he*

it
up
and
it
up
and
it
up
and
it
up
went

And hopped away proper
As any grasshopper.

David McCord

Calico Pie

I

Calico pie,
The little birds fly
Down to the calico-tree:
Their wings were blue,
And they sang "Tilly-loo!"
Till away they flew;
And they never came back to me!
They never came back,
They never came back,
They never came back to me!

II

Calico jam,
The little Fish swam
Over the Syllabub Sea.
He took off his hat
To the Sole and the Sprat,
And the Willeby-wat:
But he never came back to me;
He never came back,
He never came back,
He never came back to me.

III

Calico ban,
The little Mice ran
To be ready in time for tea;
Flippity flup,
They drank it all up,
And danced in the cup:
But they never came back to me;
They never came back,
They never came back,
They never came back to me.

IV

Calico drum,
The Grasshoppers come,
The Butterfly, Beetle, and Bee,
Over the ground,
Around and round,
With a hop and a bound;
But they never came back,
They never came back,
They never came back,
They never came back to me.

Edward Lear

Solitude

I have a house where I go
    When there's too many people,
I have a house where I go
    Where no one can be;
I have a house where I go,
Where nobody ever says "No";
Where no one says anything—so
    There is no one but me.

A. A. Milne

Blum

Dog means dog
And cat means cat;
And there are lots
Of words like that.

A cart's a cart
To pull or shove,
A plate's a plate
To eat off of.

But there are other
Words I say
When I am left
Alone to play.

Blum is one.
Blum is a word
That very few
Have ever heard.

I like to say it,
"Blum, blum, blum"—
I do it loud
Or in a hum.

All by itself
It's nice to sing:
It does not mean
A single thing.

Dorothy Aldis

Circles

The things to draw with compasses
Are suns and moons and circleses
And rows of humptydumpasses
Or anything in circuses
Like hippopotamusseses
And hoops and camels' humpasses
And wheels on clownses busseses
And fat old elephumpasses.

Harry Behn

Keziah

I have a secret place to go.
Not anyone may know.

And sometimes when the wind is rough
I cannot get there fast enough.

And sometimes when my mother
Is scolding my big brother,

My secret place, it seems to me,
Is quite the only place to be.

Gwendolyn Brooks

Understanding

Sun
and rain
and wind
and storms
and thunder go together.

There has to be a little bit of each to make the
weather.

Myra Cohn Livingston

Who has seen the wind?
    Neither I nor you:
But when the leaves hang trembling
    The wind is passing thro'.

Who has seen the wind?
    Neither you nor I:
But when the trees bow down their heads
    The wind is passing by.

Christina Rossetti

from *The Wind and The Moon*

Said the Wind to the Moon, "I will blow you out;
      You stare
      In the air
      Like a ghost in a chair,
Always looking what I am about—
I hate to be watched; I'll blow you out."

George MacDonald

The Moon's the North Wind's Cooky

The Moon's the North Wind's cooky.
He bites it, day by day,
Until there's but a rim of scraps
That crumble all away.

The South Wind is a baker.
He kneads clouds in his den,
And bakes a crisp new moon *that . . . greedy*
North . . . Wind . . . eats . . . again!

Vachel Lindsay

Dilly Dilly Piccalilli
Tell me something very silly:
There was a chap his name was Bert
He ate the buttons off his shirt.

Clyde Watson

Sing a song of succotash,
A bucketful of noses.
And here is one for each of you,
To help you sniff the roses.

Arnold Lobel

Oh my goodness, oh my dear,
Sassafras & ginger beer,
Chocolate cake & apple punch:
I'm too full to eat my lunch.

Clyde Watson

"Let's Marry!" Said the Cherry

"Let's marry,"
said the cherry.

"Why me?"
said the pea.

"'Cause you're sweet,"
said the beet.

"Say you will,"
said the dill.

"Think it over,"
said the clover.

"Don't rush,"
said the squash.

"Here's your dress,"
said the cress.

"White and green,"
said the bean.

"And your cape,"
said the grape.

"Trimmed with fur,"
said the burr.

"Won't that tickle?"
said the pickle.

"Who knows?"
said the rose.

"Where's the chapel?"
said the apple.

"In Greenwich,"
said the spinach.

"We'll be there!"
said the pear.

"Wearing what?"
said the nut.

"Pants and coats,"
said the oats.

"Shoes and socks,"
said the phlox.

"Shirt and tie,"
said the rye.

"We'll look jolly,"
said the holly.

"You'll look silly,"
said the lily.

"You're crazy,"
said the daisy.

"Come, let's dine,"
said the vine.

"Yeah—let's eat!"
said the wheat.

"And get stout,"
said the sprout.

"Just wait,"
said the date.

"Who will chime?"
said the lime.

"I'll chime!"
said the thyme.

"Who will preach?"
said the peach.

"It's my turn!"
said the fern.

"You would ramble,"
said the bramble.

"Here they come!"
cried the plum.

"Start the tune!"
cried the prune.

"All together!"
cried the heather.

"Here we go!"
said the sloe.

"NOW—let's marry!"
said the cherry.

"Why me?"
said the pea.

"Oh, my gosh!"
said the squash.

"Start all over,"
said the clover.

"NO WAY!"
said the hay.

N. M. Bodecker

Gooseberry,
Juice berry,
Loose berry jam.

Spread it on crackers,
Spread it on bread,
Try not to spread it
Onto your head.

Gooseberry,
Juice berry,
Loose berry jam.

No matter how neatly
You try to bite in,
It runs like a river
Down to your chin.

Gooseberry,
Juice berry,
Loose berry jam.

Eve Merriam

Bananas and Cream

Bananas and cream,
Bananas and cream:
All we could say was
Bananas and cream.

We couldn't say fruit,
We wouldn't say cow,
We didn't say sugar—
We don't say it now.

Bananas and cream,
Bananas and cream,
All we could shout was
Bananas and cream.

We didn't say why,
We didn't say how;
We forgot it was fruit,
We forgot the old cow;
We *never* said sugar,

We only said *WOW!*

Bananas and cream,
Bananas and cream;
And all that we want is
Bananas and cream!

We didn't say dish,
We didn't say spoon;
We said not tomorrow,
But NOW and HOW SOON

Bananas and cream,
Bananas and cream?
We yelled for bananas,
Bananas and scream!

David McCord

34

Mix a pancake,
Stir a pancake,
        Pop it in the pan;
Fry the pancake,
Toss the pancake,—
        Catch it if you can.

Christina Rossetti

If you were a pot
And I were a pan,
We could sit on the shelf together.
If you were a mountain
And I were the snow,
We wouldn't much mind the weather.

Arnold Lobel

April Rain Song

Let the rain kiss you.
Let the rain beat upon your head with silver
      liquid drops.
Let the rain sing you a lullaby.

The rain makes still pools on the sidewalk.
The rain makes running pools in the gutter.
The rain plays a little sleep-song on our roof at
      night—

And I love the rain.

Langston Hughes

April

Rain is good
for washing leaves
and stones and bricks and
even eyes,
and if you hold
your head just so
you can almost see
the tops of skies.

Lucille Clifton

It rains and it pours.
I've got too many chores,
There's the cooking and cleaning to do.
I'd rather be out on a wet, green hill,
Laughing and dancing with you.

Arnold Lobel

The Owl and The Pussy-Cat

The Owl and the Pussy-Cat went to sea
    In a beautiful pea-green boat:
They took some honey, and plenty of money
    Wrapped up in a five-pound note.
The Owl looked up to the stairs above,
    And sang to a small guitar,
    "O lovely Pussy, O Pussy, my love,
What a beautiful Pussy you are,
        You are,
        You are!
What a beautiful Pussy you are!"

Pussy said to the Owl, "You elegant fowl,
    How charmingly sweet you sing!
Oh! let us be married; too long we have tarried:
    But what shall we do for a ring?"
They sailed away, for a year and a day,
    To the land where the bong-tree grows;
And there in a wood a Piggy-wig stood,
    With a ring at the end of his nose,
        His nose,
        His nose,
    With a ring at the end of his nose.

"Dear Pig, are you willing to sell for one shilling
Your ring?" Said the Piggy, "I will."
So they took it away, and were married next day
By the Turkey who lives on the hill.
They dined on mince and slices of quince,
Which they ate with a runcible spoon;
And hand in hand, on the edge of the sand
They danced by the light of the moon,
The moon,
The moon,
They danced by the light of the moon.

Edward Lear

Little Bush

A SONG

A little bush
At the picnic place,
A little bush could talk to me.

I ran away
And hid myself,
And I found a bush that could talk to me,
A smooth little bush said a word to me.

Elizabeth Madox Roberts

Potomac Town in February

The bridge says: Come across, try me; see how
    good I am.
The big rock in the river says: Look at me;
    learn how to stand up.
The white water says: I go on; around, under,
    over, I go on.
A kneeling, scraggly pine says: I am here yet;
    they nearly got me last year.
A sliver of moon slides by on a high wind calling:
    I know why; I'll see you tomorrow; I'll tell
    you everything tomorrow.

Carl Sandburg

Snail

Snail upon the wall,
Have you got at all
Anything to tell
About your shell?

Only this, my child—
When the wind is wild,
Or when the sun is hot,
It's all I've got.

John Drinkwater

Yellow Weed

How did you get here,
weed?
Who brought your seed?

Did it lift
on the wind and
sail
and drift
from a far and yellow
field?

Was your seed a
burr,
a sticky burr that
clung to a
fox's
furry tail?

Did it fly with a
bird
who liked to feed
on the tasty
seed
of the yellow
weed?

How did you come?

Lilian Moore

45

Who?

Who's been
criss-
crossing
this
fresh snow?

Well, Rabbit was here.
How did he go?
Hop-hopping.
Stopping.
Hopping away.

A deer
stood near
this tall young tree.
Took three steps.
(What did she see?)
Didn't stay.
(What did she hear?)

Fox brushed snow dust
from a bush.
Squirrel, too.
But who—
WHO
walked on TWO legs
here
today?

Lilian Moore

46

A Small Discovery

Father,
Where do giants go to cry?

To the hills
Behind the thunder?
Or to the waterfall?
I wonder.

(Giants cry.
I know they do.
Do they wait
Till nighttime too?)

James A. Emanuel

To a Squirrel at Kyle-Na-No

Come play with me;
Why should you run
Through the shaking tree
As though I'd a gun
To strike you dead?
When all I would do
Is to scratch your head
And let you go.

William Butler Yeats

River Winding

Rain falling, what things do you grow?
Snow melting, where do you go?
Wind blowing, what trees do you know?
River winding, where do you flow?

Charlotte Zolotow

I'd Like to Be a Lighthouse

I'd like to be a lighthouse
    All scrubbed and painted white.
I'd like to be a lighthouse
    And stay awake all night
To keep my eye on everything
    That sails my patch of sea;
I'd like to be a lighthouse
    With the ships all watching me.

Rachel Field

Row, row, row
to Oyster Bay.
What sort of fish
shall we catch today?
Big fish,
small fish,
snook or snail,
yellow snapper,
triple tail,
herring
daring,
kipper
coarse,
or a trout
with applesauce?

N. M. Bodecker

At the Sea-Side

When I was down beside the sea
A wooden spade they gave to me
    To dig the sandy shore.

My holes were empty like a cup.
In every hole the sea came up
    Till it could come no more.

Robert Louis Stevenson

Old Man Ocean

Old Man Ocean, how do you pound
Smooth glass rough, rough stones round?
Time and the tide and the wild waves rolling,
Night and the wind and the long gray dawn.

Old Man Ocean, what do you tell,
What do you sing in the empty shell?
Fog and the storm and the long bell tolling,
Bones in the deep and the brave men gone.

Russell Hoban

The Little Turtle

There was a little turtle.
He lived in a box.
He swam in a puddle.
He climbed on the rocks.

He snapped at a mosquito.
He snapped at a flea.
He snapped at a minnow.
And he snapped at me.

He caught the mosquito.
He caught the flea.
He caught the minnow.
But he didn't catch me.

Vachel Lindsay

This Is My Rock

This is my rock,
And here I run
To steal the secret of the sun;

This is my rock,
And here come I
Before the night has swept the sky;

This is my rock,
This is the place
I meet the evening face to face.

David McCord

The Hens

The night was coming very fast;
It reached the gate as I ran past.

The pigeons had gone to the tower of the church
And all the hens were on their perch,

Up in the barn, and I thought I heard
A piece of a little purring word.

I stopped inside, waiting and staying,
To try to hear what the hens were saying.

They were asking something, that was plain,
Asking it over and over again.

One of them moved and turned around,
Her feathers made a ruffled sound,

A ruffled sound, like a bushful of birds,
And she said her little asking words.

She pushed her head close into her wing,
But nothing answered anything.

Elizabeth Madox Roberts

Moon

Moon
Have you met my mother?
Asleep in a chair there
Falling down hair.

Moon in the sky
Moon in the water
Have you met one another?
Moon face to moon face
Deep in that dark place
Suddenly bright.

Moon
Have you met my friend the night?

Karla Kuskin

Some One

Some one came knocking
   At my wee, small door;
Some one came knocking,
   I'm sure—sure—sure;
I listened, I opened,
   I looked to left and right,
But nought there was a-stirring
   In the still dark night;
Only the busy beetle
   Tap-tapping in the wall,
Only from the forest
   The screech-owl's call,
Only the cricket whistling
   While the dewdrops fall,
So I know not who came knocking,
   At all, at all, at all.

Walter de la Mare

The Night

The night
    creeps in
    around my head
    and snuggles down
    upon the bed
    and makes lace pictures
    on the wall
    but doesn't say a word at all.

Myra Cohn Livingston

How Far

How far
How far
How far is today
When tomorrow has come
And it's yesterday?

Far
And far
And far away.

Mary Ann Hoberman

The Question

People always say to me
"What do you think you'd like to be
When you grow up?"
And I say "Why,
I think I'd like to be the sky
Or be a plane or train or mouse
Or maybe be a haunted house
Or something furry, rough and wild . . .
Or maybe I will stay a child."

Karla Kuskin

Index of Authors

Index of Titles

Index of First Lines